LØNE K
ANOTHER SOLO RPG

KWAIDAN!
ADVENTURE PACK

ZOTIQUEST GAMES

Loner - Kwaidan!

(CC) 2023 Roberto Bisceglie

Hey there, fellow adventurers! So, you might be wondering what this whole "Kwaidan" thing is, right? Well, get ready to step into a world of Japanese folklore like no other. Kwaidan is all about immersing yourself in a realm where ghosts, demons, and all sorts of mysterious creatures roam free. And guess what? It's a perfect match for our Loner Adventure Pack. Let me break it down for you.

Picture feudal Japan, a time of warring clans and hidden supernatural forces. It's like history and the supernatural decided to have a really intriguing party together. Kwaidan stories are like those spine-tingling tales you'd share around a campfire, but with a twist: samurais, peasants, and nobles grappling with things that go bump in the night.

Now, why is Kwaidan just right for those lone wolf characters? Well, think about it—loners have that extra touch of independence, right? They're the heroes who face the unknown solo, relying on their skills and uncovering mysteries that'd make others run for the hills. And in a world full of yokai (those shape-shifting critters) and spirits looking for trouble, loners are in for some serious action, banishing, and battling.

Kwaidan isn't just about spooky stuff; it's like a cultural journey through Japan's traditions, superstitions, and beliefs. You'll find yourself sipping tea in serene gardens, exploring the ins and outs of samurai and merchants, and keeping your cool while dealing with cursed artifacts and eerie shrines. Oh, and did I mention you might stumble upon secretive ninja clans and even have run-ins with mischievous tanuki? Yup, it's that wild.

So, if you're all about getting lost in worlds where reality and the supernatural mingle, Kwaidan is your go-to. And in our Loner Adventure Pack, you'll be the star of your very own spooky saga. Get ready for a journey where courage, smarts, and a sprinkle of the unknown can lead to epic challenges and victories. Kwaidan's here to whisk you away to a land where the unseen is waiting for you to uncover.

SETTING INFORMATION

- **Feudal Japan Amidst Conflict:** The stage is set in feudal Japan, a tumultuous era marked by the clash of warring clans. The land is steeped in political strife, where power struggles and territorial disputes are commonplace. Against this backdrop of unrest, something even more sinister stirs – shadowy supernatural forces that wield their own influence over the fate of the land.

- **Vulnerability of Remote Villages and Travelers:** Beyond the bustling cities and grand castles, the rural landscapes hide isolated villages and winding, lonely roads. As night falls, these places become particularly vulnerable to the unknown. Stories of eerie occurrences and unexplained phenomena abound, creating an atmosphere of tension and unease. The veil between the material world and the supernatural is thin in these desolate reaches, making them prime locations for encounters with otherworldly entities.

- **A World of Mystery and Danger:** The natural world is both breathtakingly beautiful and perilous in equal measure. Mist-shrouded forests, misty mountains, and hidden valleys hold untold mysteries, many of which are as dangerous as they are enchanting. Ancient legends and whispered tales warn of malevolent spirits lurking in the shadows, waiting to ensnare unsuspecting souls. Navigating this world requires not only physical prowess but also a keen understanding of the arcane.

- **Stratified Social Hierarchy:** Feudal society is deeply stratified, with a rigid social hierarchy dictating the roles and statuses of its inhabitants. At the pinnacle stand the revered samurai warriors and noble class, shaping the course of events with their political maneuvering and martial prowess. Beneath them, peasants and merchants toil, their lives governed by the decisions of those above. This stark division of power and influence has far-reaching implications for every facet of life in this era.

- **Influence of Folklore and Superstition:** The realm of superstition and folklore is interwoven into the very fabric of everyday existence. The beliefs and tales passed down through generations shape the perceptions and actions of individuals. Ghostly apparitions, demonic entities, and creatures that can transform from one form to another are not simply fantastical imaginings but tangible aspects of this world. Fear of the unknown and reverence for the spiritual underscore every interaction and decision.

- **Historical Landmarks and Turmoil:** The tumultuous history of the land is etched into its very soil. The echoes of pivotal battles and the rise of powerful warlords reverberate through the years, creating a sense of both grandeur and foreboding. Majestic castles and legendary battlegrounds serve as reminders of the struggles that have defined the era. Exploring these landmarks not only offers insight into the past but also a chance to uncover hidden truths that can illuminate the present challenges faced by the land.

THEMES

These thematic elements can add depth, complexity, and emotional resonance to the setting, providing with engaging narratives that reflect the richness of feudal Japan.

- **Balance of Light and Darkness**: Explore the duality of light and darkness, both in the physical world and within characters' motivations. Delve into the struggle between good and evil, and the shades of gray that exist in between.

- **Spiritual Warfare:** Dive into the realm of the supernatural and delve into battles against malevolent spirits, learning the rituals, charms, and incantations necessary to protect oneself and banish these entities.

- **Fear and Courage:** Delve into the theme of fear, and the different ways characters cope with and overcome it. The concept of facing one's deepest fears and finding courage within oneself can be a central narrative thread.

- **Cultural Traditions:** Immerse yourself in the cultural traditions of feudal Japan, from tea ceremonies and calligraphy to samurai codes and societal expectations. Encourage characters to navigate these traditions while facing the challenges of the supernatural world.

- **Personal Redemption:** Provide opportunities for characters to seek redemption for past mistakes, either through helping spirits find peace or rectifying wrongs committed by their ancestors.

- **Forgotten Memories:** Characters could uncover forgotten memories tied to the past, leading them to confront ancient conflicts or hidden truths that have repercussions in the present.

- **Finding Closure:** Many spirits are trapped due to unfinished business. Characters could embark on quests to help these spirits find closure and move on to the afterlife.

- **The Power of Words and Symbols:** Introduce the idea that certain words, symbols, and rituals can have profound effects on the supernatural world, acting as tools for protection, exorcism, or even manipulation.

- **Perception vs. Reality:** Challenge characters to question their perceptions and decipher illusions. This theme can be particularly relevant when dealing with shapeshifting creatures and deceitful spirits.

- **Respect for Nature:** Emphasize the reverence for nature in Japanese culture and its potential consequences when disregarded. Characters might need to restore balance to natural elements disrupted by supernatural forces.

CONCEPTS

	⚀	⚁	⚂
⚀	Disgraced Samurai	Masterless Ronin	Peasant Farmer
⚁	Haunted Widow	Demon Hunter	Wandering Priest
⚂	Unfortunate Orphan	Troubled Monk	Ronin Swordsman
⚃	Cursed Artist	Wandering Exorcist	Haunted Samurai
⚄	Troubled Medic	Possessed Shapeshifter	Ronin Bodyguard
⚅	Wandering Exorcist	Peasant Guide	Cursed Samurai

	⚃	⚄	⚅
⚀	Mendicant Monk	Travelling Minstrel	Disfigured Ronin
⚁	Unfortunate Merchant	Possessed Child	Cursed Warrior
⚂	Wandering Minstrel	Troubled Alchemist	Possessed Woodsman
⚃	Unfortunate Orphan	Disgraced Warrior	Wandering Mendicant
⚄	Unfortunate Daimyo	Troubled Farmer	Disfigured Diviner
⚅	Demon Hunter	Possessed Child	Troubled Monk

SKILLS

	⚀	⚁	⚂
⚀	Swordplay	Stealth	Horsemanship
⚁	Archery	Spiritualism	Etiquette
⚂	Athletics	Intimidation	Animal Handling
⚃	Persuasion	Deception	Investigation
⚄	Unarmed Combat	Mind Resistance	Exorcism
⚅	Shapeshifting	Invisibility	Telepathy
	⚃	⚄	⚅
⚀	Hunting	Survival	Medicine
⚁	Tea Ceremony	Ikebana	Divination
⚂	Engineering	Agriculture	Lore
⚃	Perception	Crafting	Artistry
⚄	Kenjutsu	Metallurgy	Mountaineering
⚅	Telekinesis	Pyromancy	Necromancy

FRAILTIES

	⚀	⚁	⚂
⚀	Possessed	Cowardly	Agoraphobic
⚁	Haunted	Superstitious	Reckless
⚂	Cursed	Addicted	Prejudiced
⚃	Schizophrenic	Alcoholic	Pyromaniac
⚄	Narcissistic	Bipolar	Deceitful
⚅	Obsessive	Suicidal	Insomniac
	⚃	⚄	⚅
⚀	Dishonored	Vengeful	Paranoid
⚁	Depressive	Proud	Schizophrenic
⚂	Obsessive	Traumatized	Mute
⚃	Compulsive	Masochistic	Suicidal
⚄	Sadistic	Kleptomanic	Amnesiac
⚅	Narcoleptic	Greedy	Sickly

GEAR

	⚀	⚁	⚂
⚀	Katana	Wakizashi	Tanto
⚁	Lantern	Medicine	Kimono
⚂	Horses	Oxen	Cart
⚃	Ofuda	Shakujo	Rosary
⚄	Armor	Tekko	Naginata
⚅	Bombs	Poison	Net
	⚃	⚄	⚅
⚀	Bow	Arrows	Spear
⚁	Sandals	Tatami	Backpack
⚂	Boat	Tent	Cooking
⚃	Mask	Tobacco	Sake
⚄	B¶	Tetsubo	Shuriken
⚅	Chains	Manriki	Smokebomb

FEMALE

	⚀	⚁	⚂
⚀	Akari	Hana	Yuki
⚁	Emiko	Aiko	Sakura
⚂	Ayame	Yumiko	Natsuki
⚃	Keiko	Rei	Asuka
⚄	Amaya	Eri	Kana
⚅	Yui	Nozomi	Hinata
	⚃	⚄	⚅
⚀	Mei	Sora	Kaori
⚁	Rina	Kiyomi	Mika
⚂	Aya	Haruka	Kimiko
⚃	Natsumi	Yuri	Chieko
⚄	Misaki	Tomoko	Ayumi
⚅	Yuna	Akane	Nanami

MALE

	⚀	⚁	⚂
⚀	Ren	Hiroshi	Kaito
⚁	Kenji	Kazuki	Ryota
⚂	Satoshi	Yuki	Riku
⚃	Naoki	Akihiro	Kenta
⚄	Kaito	Taro	Yuma
⚅	Renji	Junichi	Taichi

	⚃	⚄	⚅
⚀	Takashi	Haruki	Daiki
⚁	Tatsuya	Yuto	Akihiko
⚂	Makoto	Sora	Shinji
⚃	Sho	Toshiro	Haruto
⚄	Ryo	Keisuke	Hayato
⚅	Shota	Hiroto	Sosuke

SURNAMES

	⚀	⚁	⚂
⚀	Tanaka	Yamamoto	Suzuki
⚁	Nakamura	Kobayashi	Kato
⚂	Okada	Sakamoto	Inoue
⚃	Mori	Ishikawa	Otsuka
⚄	Aoki	Ogawa	Matsumoto
⚅	Hasegawa	Nakanishi	Taniguchi

	⚃	⚄	⚅
⚀	Watanabe	Itou	Sato
⚁	Takahashi	Ito	Abe
⚂	Kimura	Hayashi	Yamada
⚃	Nishimura	Fujita	Sasaki
⚄	Suzuki	Ikeda	Morita
⚅	Saito	Hayashi	Shibata

SETTLEMENTS

	⚀	⚁	⚂
⚀	Mizukaze	Hoshizora	Yamanami
⚁	Inari	Himawari	Suzaku
⚂	Kurogane	Mizuhara	Sakura
⚃	Kamimizu	Komorebi	Aozora
⚄	Kazan	Yukizuki	Akane
⚅	Isogai	Miharashi	Tachibana

	⚃	⚄	⚅
⚀	Akatsuki	Kasumi	Kiyomizu
⚁	Yamabiko	Shizuka	Tsukinami
⚂	Hayabusa	Amagumo	Fujimori
⚃	Yamashiro	Ayatsuri	Shinrin
⚄	Hotarubi	Kageyama	Utsukushi
⚅	Nijigami	Yurei	Minakami

REGIONS

	⚀	⚁	⚂
⚀	Higashima	Nishizora	Minakami
⚁	Kizan	Yamanomi	Kanazawa
⚂	Kiso	Kansai	Shikoku
⚃	Shonan	Hokuriku	Hokkaido
⚄	Aomori	Chubu	Tokai
⚅	Iwate	Kanto	Shikoku

	⚃	⚄	⚅
⚀	Okuizumo	Kochi	Kumamoto
⚁	Chugoku	Boso	Yamagata
⚂	Tohoku	Chubu	Kyushu
⚃	Chugoku	Izu	Kyushu
⚄	Tohoku	Ogasawara	Okinawa
⚅	Kyushu	Kii	Akita

LOCATIONS

	⚀	⚁	⚂
⚀	Hikari	Kaguya	Ryuji
⚁	Izanagi	Amaterasu	Uzume
⚂	Enma	Tenjin	Akatsuki
⚃	Fujin	Raijin	Izanami
⚄	Marishiten	Kujaku	Susano'o
⚅	Uka	Miroku	Asura

	⚃	⚄	⚅
⚀	Amano	Tsukuyomi	Seiryu
⚁	Shinrin	Fujin	Raijin
⚂	Kannon	Ebisu	Daikokuten
⚃	Fudo	Benzaiten	Jurojin
⚄	Gekko	Ryujin	Ame-no-Uz
⚅	Jizo	Emma	Benten

SPECIAL RULES

Consider the following as Luck-like scores, with a starting (and maximum) score of 6.

- **Chi:** Characters have a Chi score used to power supernatural abilities. Chi is drained by using abilities and recovered by meditation.
- **Corruption:** Exposure to supernatural evil can corrupt the soul. Track corruption separately from health. Those fully corrupted may become monsters.
- **Honor:** Dishonorable acts drain Honor. Without honor, samurai lose status and peasants lose hope. Regaining honor may require quests.

FACTIONS

THE SHOGUN'S FORCES

- **Concept:** Lawful Army
- **Skills:** Horsemanship, Tactics
- **Frailty:** Blind Obedience
- **Gear:** Armor, Spears
- **Goal:** Enforce the Shogun's will
- **Motive:** Loyalty and duty
- **Nemesis:** Rebels and outlaws

THE ANIMAL CULTS

- **Concept:** Savage Beast Worshippers
- **Skills:** Shapeshifting, Wilderness Survival
- **Frailty:** Bloodlust
- **Gear:** Furs, Claws
- **Goal:** Spread corruption through the land
- **Motive:** Serve their animal spirits
- **Nemesis:** Demon hunters

THE DRAGON CLAN

- **Concept:** Noble Warriors
- **Skills:** Kenjutsu, Etiquette
- **Frailty:** Pride
- **Gear:** Fine Kimono, Katana
- **Goal:** Rule justly and expand their lands
- **Motive:** Honor and duty
- **Nemesis:** Rival warlords

THE BAMBOO CUTTERS

- **Concept:** Peasant Rebels
- **Skills:** Sabotage, Stealth
- **Frailty:** Recklessness
- **Gear:** Farming Tools, Staves
- **Goal:** Oppose tyranny
- **Motive:** Justice
- **Nemesis:** Corrupt officials

THE SOHEI

- **Concept:** Militant Monks
- **Skills:** Martial Arts, Exorcism
- **Frailty:** Fanaticism
- **Gear:** Robes, Staves
- **Goal:** Battle supernatural evil
- **Motive:** Protect the innocent
- **Nemesis:** Demons and cultists

THE SHADOW WALKER CLAN

- **Concept:** Mercenary Ninjas
- **Skills:** Stealth, Poison
- **Frailty:** Greed
- **Gear:** Black Clothes, Ninja Gear
- **Goal:** Get paid
- **Motive:** Money and influence
- **Nemesis:** Those who don't pay them

NPCS

DAIMYO AKIRA

- **Concept:** Ambitious Warlord
- **Skills:** Tactics, Intimidation
- **Frailty:** Wrath
- **Gear:** Armor, Katana
- **Goal:** Conquer more lands
- **Motive:** Greed and pride
- **Nemesis:** Rival warlords

PEASANT GIRL HANAKO

- **Concept:** Cursed Youth
- **Skills:** Farming, Animal Handling
- **Frailty:** Haunted
- **Gear:** Straw Hat, Kimono
- **Goal:** Break her curse
- **Motive:** Anguish over her condition
- **Nemesis:** The demon who cursed her

RONIN TAKA

- **Concept:** Disgraced Swordsman
- **Skills:** Kenjutsu, Gambling
- **Frailty:** Dishonored
- **Gear:** Katana, Flask of Sake
- **Goal:** Regain his honor
- **Motive:** Shame and regret
- **Nemesis:** Those who know of his disgrace

PRIESTESS YURI

- **Concept:** Veteran Exorcist
- **Skills:** Exorcism, Spiritualism
- **Frailty:** World-weariness
- **Gear:** Rosary, Robes
- **Goal:** Cleanse the land of evil
- **Motive:** Protect the innocent
- **Nemesis:** The forces of corruption

TANUKI SHAPESHIFTER ROKU

- **Concept:** Mischievous Trickster
- **Skills:** Shapeshift-ing, Deception
- **Frailty:** Greed
- **Gear:** Magical Leaf
- **Goal:** Create harm-less chaos
- **Motive:** Boredom and amusement
- **Nemesis:** Those who don't enjoy his pranks

MERCHANT LORD HIROSHI

- **Concept:** Shrewd Trade Magnate
- **Skills:** Persuasion, Deception
- **Frailty:** Greed
- **Gear:** Ornate Kimono, Silk Sash
- **Goal:** Expand his trade network
- **Motive:** Wealth and power
- **Nemesis:** Rival merchants

LOCATIONS

THE HOWLING FOREST
- The trees are ancient and gnarled. Strange screams echo at night.
- **Possible encounters:** Demon, bandits, ghost, tanuki, hunter, old temple

THE CURSED HOT SPRINGS
- Once a place of relaxation, now the waters are blackened.
- **Possible encounters:** Cursed spirit, sick villagers, kappa, abandoned inn, traveling minstrel

THE FORGOTTEN SHRINE
- This old shrine is half-collapsed and overgrown. Locals avoid it.
- **Possible encounters:** Angry ghost, kappa, mujina, old priest, occult artifacts

THE EASTERN ROAD
- This remote road winds through the mountains. Travelers often disappear along it.
- **Possible encounters:** Bandits, nurikabe, possessed traveler, merchant caravan, ghostly procession

THE FOGGY MOORS
- These moors are cloaked in unnatural fog. Strange lights are seen at night.
- **Possible encounters:** Yokai, will-o-wisps, cursed travelers, abandoned manor, insane artist

THE SINGING CAVE
- Local legends tell of a cave that drives those who hear its eerie songs insane.
- **Possible encounters:** Demons, possessed hermit, giant bats, ancient scrolls, ghostly singers

HAUNTED ARTIFACTS

D66	Haunted Artifact
11	**Whispering Blade:** This ancient katana holds the souls of fallen warriors, granting it deadly power in battle. But beware, for its whispers can drive the wielder to madness.
12	**Mask of Shadows:** When worn, this mask grants the ability to see in darkness and become unseen. However, it also feeds off your inner fears, slowly draining your courage.
13	**Amulet of Protection:** A shimmering amulet that shields you from harm. But every time it saves you, it demands a small token in return – a memory or an emotion.
14	**Bamboo Flute of Tranquility:** A haunting melody can be played on this flute, soothing minds and healing hearts. Yet its soothing tunes can also attract spirits from the beyond.
15	**Stone of Reflection:** Gaze into this polished stone and see visions of the past or glimpse into the future. But be warned, these visions might come at a price.
16	**Fan of Galeforce:** With a flick of this fan, you can summon mighty winds to clear your path. Yet its power might also bring forth storms and chaos.
21	**Teacup of Clarity:** Sipping tea from this cup grants insight and wisdom. But each sip connects you to the spirits of those who drank from it before.
22	**Cursed Compass:** This compass points the way to hidden treasures. But it's cursed – the more you rely on it, the more it leads you astray.
23	**Shroud of Invisibility:** Wrap yourself in this shroud to become invisible to the world. Yet the longer you remain hidden, the more you risk losing touch with reality.
24	**Scroll of Binding:** A scroll that can bind and control supernatural creatures. However, each binding costs a fragment of your life force.
25	**Bell of Warning:** Ring this bell to alert you to danger. But it also warns nearby spirits of your presence, inviting their attention.
26	**Mirror of Truth:** Gaze into this mirror to see through illusions and deceit. Yet its truth can be harsh, revealing more than you may want to know.

D66	Haunted Artifact
31	**Sake Cup of Valor:** Drinking from this cup grants courage and strength. But its effects are fleeting, and the price is a deep and lasting fatigue.
32	**Earring of Eavesdropping:** Wear this earring to hear distant conversations. Yet the more secrets you uncover, the more your own thoughts might be exposed.
33	**Lantern of Lost Souls:** This lantern illuminates the spirit world, revealing hidden truths. But it also attracts restless spirits who seek your aid.
34	**Sealing Scroll:** A scroll that can seal away supernatural forces. But the more you use it, the more it drains your vitality.
35	**Mirror of Vanity:** Gaze into this mirror to temporarily enhance your appearance and charisma. But vanity comes at a cost – it feeds on your self-esteem.
36	**Cursed Quill:** Writing with this quill brings your words to life. However, the quill craves dark stories, and your creations might have unintended consequences.
41	**Stone of Echoes:** Whisper a message into this stone, and it will carry your words across distances. But your own secrets might also be revealed.
42	**Ring of Fortune:** Wear this ring for a stroke of luck in your endeavors. Yet it tempts fate – the more you rely on it, the more danger it attracts.
43	**Ink of Enchantment:** This ink imbues your drawings with magic, bringing them to life. But the more intricate the drawing, the greater the toll on your energy.
44	**Compass of Lost Souls:** This compass guides you to those who are lost. But with each guiding, you risk becoming lost yourself.
45	**Fang of the Beast:** This fang grants the strength and instincts of a wild beast. Yet its primal power might consume your human nature.
46	**Chalice of Dreams:** Sip from this chalice to experience vivid dreams that might reveal insights. But these dreams can blur the line between reality and illusion.

D66	Haunted Artifact
51	**Mask of Deception:** A mask that grants the power of deception, making you appear as someone else. However, the mask might also blur your own identity.
52	**Brazier of Protection:** This brazier wards off evil spirits with its holy flames. But the stronger its protection, the more it demands your devotion.
53	**Rune-etched Bracelet:** Wear this bracelet to channel elemental magic. But its runes can also bind you to the elements, leaving you vulnerable.
54	**Mirror of Regret:** Gaze into this mirror to witness past events and seek understanding. But dwelling on regrets might trap you in a cycle of despair.
55	**Cursed Dice:** Roll these dice to alter fate itself. Yet their power can backfire, leading to unexpected and dire consequences.
56	**Stone of Levitation:** Touch this stone to defy gravity and levitate. But the longer you remain airborne, the more you risk losing touch with the ground.
61	**Scroll of Illusions:** Unroll this scroll to create illusions that deceive the senses. But illusions can twist your perception, leading you astray.
62	**Bell of Tranquility:** Ring this bell to bring calm and serenity to chaotic situations. Yet its peaceful aura might also attract restless spirits.
63	**Talisman of Warding:** Wear this talisman for protection against supernatural forces. But as its power grows, it might draw these forces to you.
64	**Veil of Dreams:** This veil allows you to enter the dreams of others. But navigating dreams comes with its own risks and mysteries.
65	**Mask of Revelations:** A mask that reveals hidden truths and secrets. Yet truth can be a double-edged sword, sometimes better left unsaid.
66	**Elixir of Euphoria:** Drinking this elixir grants moments of pure joy and ecstasy. But its intoxicating effects might lead you down a dangerous path.

MYSTICAL LOCATIONS

D66	Mystical Location
11	**Veiled Forest:** This forest is shrouded in a perpetual mist, obscuring ancient trees and forgotten ruins. Beware the spirits that drift among the veiled trees.
12	**Forgotten Shrine:** An old shrine lies in ruins, its sacred grounds abandoned and overgrown. Yet whispers of prayers and distant echoes linger here.
13	**Caverns of Echoes:** These echoing caverns play tricks on sound, distorting voices and cries. Rumor has it, those who listen closely might hear the secrets of the earth.
14	**Ephemeral Pond:** A tranquil pond that reflects the moon's glow. Legend says it's a gateway to the spirit world, but those who linger too long risk becoming trapped.
15	**Lost Garden:** An ornate garden once tended by spirits, now overgrown and forgotten. Its flowers still bloom, but they respond to the whispers of those who visit.
16	**Haunting Hollow:** A natural amphitheater surrounded by ancient stone columns. Eerie music fills the air as if the stones themselves are singing.
21	**Cursed Marshlands:** A desolate marsh where the land seems to shift beneath your feet. Ghostly lights dance above the marsh's surface, luring unwary travelers.
22	**Whispering Woods:** The trees here bear secrets whispered by the wind. Listen closely and you might glean ancient tales or cryptic warnings.
23	**Spectral Ruins:** The remains of an ancient city, now inhabited by spirits and shadows. The spirits might offer wisdom, but their intentions are often inscrutable.
24	**Enchanted Waterfall:** A waterfall that shimmers with otherworldly hues. Those who bathe in its waters might be granted visions of the past or glimpses of the future.
25	**Haunted Manor:** An abandoned manor rumored to be haunted. Echoes of laughter and music can still be heard, and its halls are said to be trapped in a time loop.
26	**Luminous Lagoon:** A lagoon that glows with an ethereal light at night. Its waters are said to reveal hidden truths to those who gaze upon them.

D66	Mystical Location
31	**Moonlit Bridge:** A bridge that materializes only under the light of the full moon, spanning across a chasm. It leads to a realm that exists only in moonlit hours.
32	**Eerie Echo Cave:** A cave known for its unusual acoustics. Words spoken here are carried throughout the cavern, sometimes distorting their meaning.
33	**Sorrowful Grove:** A grove of trees that weep translucent tears. Drinking these tears grants visions, but also leaves a mark on the drinker's soul.
34	**Temple of Whispers:** A serene temple where wind whispers through the corridors. Visitors might gain guidance from the whispers of ancient spirits.
35	**Mystic Mirage Oasis:** An oasis that appears and disappears like a mirage. Its waters can heal wounds, but the oasis can be elusive and hard to find.
36	**Labyrinthine Passage:** A network of underground passages filled with puzzles and riddles. Solving them might lead to hidden chambers of forgotten knowledge.
41	**Spectral Bridge:** A bridge spanning a river said to be the boundary between the living and spirit worlds. Those who cross it might experience strange visions.
42	**Frozen Temple:** A temple enveloped in an eternal winter. Its icy halls are home to both spirits seeking refuge and those guarding its sacred knowledge.
43	**Silent Monoliths:** Tall stone monoliths that emit a faint hum. Those who listen closely might hear echoes of conversations from long ago.
44	**Celestial Observatory:** An ancient observatory atop a mountain, where celestial events can reveal hidden paths and truths to those who watch the skies.
45	**Tranquil Sanctuary:** A hidden sanctuary untouched by time, where the spirits of nature gather. Meditating here can offer insight into the world's balance.
46	**Ethereal Falls:** A waterfall that cascades upward, defying gravity. Its waters grant a temporary ability to walk on air, but not without risks.

D66	Mystical Location
51	**Veil of Illusions:** A misty vale where illusions come to life. Navigating through the illusions might reveal hidden treasures or reveal one's true nature.
52	**Echoing Chamber:** A chamber where sound reverberates endlessly. Utter a question, and the chamber might provide an answer – but its wisdom is cryptic.
53	**Glowing Grove:** A grove of trees that emit a soft glow at night. Those who rest beneath their branches might experience vivid dreams.
54	**Mystic Mirage Dunes:** A desert that shimmers with mirages. Those who navigate through the illusions might find an oasis of truth in the sands.
55	**Enigmatic Standing Stones:** A circle of standing stones that hum with an otherworldly energy. They can reveal hidden pathways to those who touch them.
56	**Lost Lighthouse:** A lighthouse that guides lost ships through the fog. Its keeper is rumored to possess ancient knowledge of the sea.
61	**Starlit Cave:** A cave illuminated only by the luminescence of crystals. Its walls depict star patterns that can provide guidance to lost travelers.
62	**Whispering Grotto:** A coastal grotto where the sea breeze carries whispers of the tides. Those who listen closely might gain insights into the future.
63	**Mystic Mirage Oasis:** An oasis that appears and disappears like a mirage. Its waters can heal wounds, but the oasis can be elusive and hard to find.
64	**Eerie Echo Canyon:** A canyon that seems to amplify sounds. Each echo reveals a faint message from the past, creating an eerie symphony.
65	**Cursed Catacombs:** An underground labyrinth where restless spirits dwell. Each turn might lead to a hidden treasure or a spectral encounter.
66	**Hidden Lotus Garden:** A garden where the lotus flowers bloom only during a specific alignment of the stars. The pollen can bring visions, but also unsettling dreams.

RANDOM EVENTS

D66	Random Event
11	**Spirit Lanterns:** Wisps of light lead you off the path to a glade where ghostly lanterns sway. Do you follow?
12	**Sudden Fog:** A thick fog engulfs you, concealing all but the immediate surroundings. Navigating becomes treacherous.
13	**Celestial Omen:** A shooting star streaks across the night sky. Some believe it foretells an upcoming event.
14	**Mysterious Footprints:** Unusual footprints lead into the forest. Following them might lead to unexpected discoveries.
15	**Friendly Yokai:** A playful yokai offers assistance or guidance. But yokai motives are often more complex than they seem.
16	**Thunderstorm:** Dark clouds gather, and thunder rumbles ominously. Seek shelter or brave the tempest?
21	**Spectral Music:** Melodic music drifts on the wind. Following it leads to a hidden grove where spirits dance.
22	**Startling Encounter:** You stumble upon a solitary figure deep in thought. They seem to have been waiting for someone.
23	**Curious Artifact:** An odd object catches your eye, half-buried in the earth. What secrets does it hold?
24	**Benevolent Guardian:** A mysterious figure watches over your campsite during the night. Their intentions are unclear.
25	**Haunted Whispers:** Faint voices echo in your ears, revealing cryptic riddles or snippets of forgotten tales.
26	**Flowering Shadows:** An ancient tree's blossoms cast intricate patterns on the ground. The petals hold power... or danger.

D66	Random Event
31	**Strange Animal:** An animal behaves unusually, leading you on a detour. Is it trying to warn you, or is it just an animal?
32	**Moonlit Encounter:** An ethereal figure emerges from the moonlit shadows, offering guidance or a cryptic message.
33	**Blossom Storm:** Cherry blossoms fall like snow, creating a beautiful but eerie atmosphere. What lies within the petals?
34	**Mystic Mirage:** The landscape shifts before your eyes, revealing a mirrored version of reality. Step through, or stay put?
35	**Lost in Thought:** A solitary monk meditates by the roadside. Join them, and you might gain insight into your journey.
36	**Feral Guardians:** Enormous, wild creatures block your path. Are they protectors of this land, or something more sinister?
41	**Whispering Winds:** The wind carries distant voices and secrets. Follow the whispers to unravel hidden truths.
42	**Mysterious Offer:** A mysterious figure presents you with a cryptic choice that could impact your destiny.
43	**Unseen Observer:** You have the uncanny feeling of being watched. Yet, no one is visible among the trees.
44	**Blossom Trail:** A trail of cherry blossoms beckons you deeper into the forest. What awaits at the end?
45	**Guardian Statues:** A row of guardian statues seems to move and shift when you're not looking directly at them.
46	**Mischievous Spirits:** Playful spirits steal your belongings and scatter them. Retrieve your items or engage in their antics.

D66	Random Event
51	**Crying Spirits:** You hear the mournful cries of spirits, urging you to help them find peace. Will you heed their call?
52	**Freak Weather:** The weather changes drastically within moments, from sunshine to torrential rain or vice versa.
53	**Veil of Illusion:** The world around you distorts and shifts, creating illusions that could lead you astray.
54	**Lingering Echoes:** The echoes of a long-forgotten battle resound in the air, revealing hints of a tragic past.
55	**Guiding Fireflies:** Fireflies light your way in the darkness, leading you to a hidden clearing or cave.
56	**Starlit Serenade:** Stars align to form a recognizable shape, an ancient celestial map that might guide your journey.
61	**Restless Wind:** An eerie wind carries whispers of secrets and truths from distant lands. What tales does it tell?
62	**Phantom Horses:** Spectral horses appear, inviting you to join their midnight ride. Will you accept their ghostly invitation?
63	**Lost Lament:** A sorrowful song fills the air, sung by a voice you can't quite locate. Will you seek its source?
64	**Cursed Artifact:** You stumble upon an artifact bearing a malevolent aura. Will you keep it for its power, or destroy it?
65	**Guardian of Dreams:** A guardian spirit visits you in your dreams, offering advice or cryptic visions of the future.
66	**Wandering Shadows:** Eerie figures wander the forest, trailing shadows that seem disconnected from their forms. Approach with caution.

ADVENTURE SEEDS

D66	Adventure
11	A remote village is being terrorized by a mysterious creature. Track it down and destroy it.
12	An ancient demon was sealed away in a forgotten shrine. Find a way to prevent its followers from freeing it.
13	A cursed katana that possesses its wielder has fallen into the hands of a daimyo's enforcer. Retrieve it before more innocents are killed.
14	A wealthy merchant was kidnapped along the Eastern Road. Rescue the merchant from the bandits.
15	A corrupt priest is consorting with evil spirits. Expose his deeds without bringing dishonor upon the temple.
16	Peasants report seeing ghosts marching across the Foggy Moors at night. Investigate and lay the spirits to rest.
21	The waters of the Cursed Hot Springs have turned poisonous. Discover the cause and restore the waters.
22	A ronin duels you for a perceived slight and you must face him honorably. Defeat him without killing him.
23	A child from a remote village has been possessed by a demon. Find a way to exorcise the demon.
24	You are drawn into a supernatural card game in a remote inn. Win to escape, or you forfeit your soul.
25	You find a cursed mask that transforms the wearer. Keep it from harming anyone else.
26	You are hired to guide a nobleman's daughter through the dangerous Howling Forest. Keep her safe on the journey.

D66	Adventure
31	A monk monastery has been plagued by misfortune. Discover if it is human sabotage or a curse.
32	The ghost of a vengeful samurai haunts a battlefield. Discover what is keeping him from rest.
33	A shapeshifter has replaced the local daimyo. Identify the imposter and expose them.
34	The voices from the Singing Cave have driven villagers insane. Find a way to silence them.
35	A kappa has moved into the local river and is drowning people. Trick it or force it away.
36	A necromancer is raising an undead army in the mountains. Infiltrate his keep and stop the ritual.
41	You are hired to secretly escort a concubine escaping an abusive noble. Get her safely away.
42	A spy has stolen important plans and taken refuge in a remote inn. Catch him without innocent bloodshed.
43	A priest hires you to discreetly retrieve occult items stolen from his temple.
44	You are challenged to an irezumi tattoo contest by a mysterious wandering artist.
45	A samurai's prized sword was stolen by tanuki. Recover it from the tricksters.
46	You must win a dangerous race through the mountains for honor and glory.

D66	Adventure
51	You stumble upon a remote village practicing forbidden rituals. They attack rather than risk exposure.
52	A garment animated by a vengeful spirit strangles people who wear it. Track down and destroy the dangerous tsukumogami.
53	You are caught in a never-ending illusion woven by a mysterious sorcerer. Escape or be trapped forever.
54	A cursed nobleman is slowly transforming into a demonic entity. Save him or end the threat.
55	A murderer uses ninjutsu to avoid capture. You must apply cunning to bring him to justice.
56	A band of ninja attempt to assassinate you after a case of mistaken identity. Survive their attacks.
61	You must mediate a supernatural dispute between feuding animal clans.
62	A gentle bamboo cutter is revealed to be blessed with divine powers. Protect their secret identity.
63	Evil priests have abducted potential psychics to turn them into weapons. Rescue them.
64	The fantastical stories told by a traveling minstrel appear to be coming true, with dangerous consequences.
65	A cowardly samurai's ancestral sword compels him to acts of courage whether he wills it or not.
66	You seek refuge in a remote monastery, only to find the monks are not what they seem. Escape with your life.

BESTIARY

AKANAME

- **Concept:** Goblin-like spirit that licks filth
- **Skills:** Filth Manipulation, Disgusting Aura
- **Frailty:** Vulnerable to cleanliness or purification rituals
- **Gear:** Filthy hands and tongue
- **Goal:** Clean dirty spaces by licking filth
- **Motive:** Sustain itself and fulfill its purpose
- **Nemesis:** Those who keep their spaces clean or protective spirits

AKASHITA

- **Concept:** Ghostly hand beneath tatami mats
- **Skills:** Surprise Attack, Stealth
- **Frailty:** Vulnerable to light or salt
- **Gear:** Ghostly hand
- **Goal:** Startle and shock unsuspecting victims
- **Motive:** Seek amusement or surprise
- **Nemesis:** Those who seal off tatami mats or protective charms

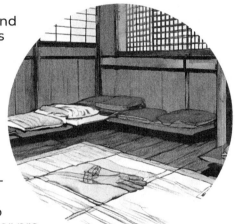

AMANOJAKU

- **Concept:** Mischievous demons causing chaos and confusion
- **Skills:** Instigation, Manipulation
- **Frailty:** Vulnerable to exorcism or divine intervention
- **Gear:** None
- **Goal:** Create discord and turmoil
- **Motive:** Seek amusement or exert control
- **Nemesis:** Individuals skilled in conflict resolution or harmony

ENENRA

- **Concept:** Creature of smoke or mist
- **Skills:** Smoke Manipulation, Intangibility
- **Frailty:** Vulnerable to strong wind or air purification
- **Gear:** None
- **Goal:** Create a smoky and eerie atmosphere
- **Motive:** Seek confusion or fear
- **Nemesis:** Air manipulators or those with smoke-resistant abilities

HITOTSUME-KOZO

- **Concept:** One-eyed monk spirit
- **Skills:** Hypnotic Gaze, Stealth
- **Frailty:** Vulnerable to salt or purification rituals
- **Gear:** None
- **Goal:** Startle and confuse humans
- **Motive:** Seek amusement or sustenance
- **Nemesis:** Those with strong willpower or mystical abilities

HIHI

- **Concept:** Creature with bird-like appearance and fire control
- **Skills:** Pyrokinesis, Fiery Aura
- **Frailty:** Vulnerable to water or fire-extinguishing methods
- **Gear:** None
- **Goal:** Manipulate and control fire for various purposes
- **Motive:** Maintain the balance of fire's destructive and creative aspects
- **Nemesis:** Water manipulators or those with fire-resistant abilities

HYAKKI YAGY¶

- **Concept:** Parade of one hundred demons and supernatural beings
- **Skills:** Collective Action, Illusion Projection
- **Frailty:** Vulnerable to disruption or dispelling magic
- **Gear:** Various youkai abilities
- **Goal:** Roam and cause chaos during the night parade
- **Motive:** Seek amusement or confusion
- **Nemesis:** Guardians of order or individuals skilled in countering illusions

JIBAKUREI

- **Concept:** Land-bound spirits attached to specific locations
- **Skills:** Manifestation, Territorial Influence
- **Frailty:** Vulnerable to purification rituals or displacement
- **Gear:** None
- **Goal:** Guard their territory and the people within
- **Motive:** Protect their domain and maintain balance
- **Nemesis:** Individuals who desecrate or disrupt their territory

JOROGUMO

- **Concept:** Seductive spider woman
- **Skills:** Shape-shifting, Deception
- **Frailty:** Vulnerable to fire or purification rituals
- **Gear:** None
- **Goal:** Lure victims and consume them
- **Motive:** Sustain themselves through deception
- **Nemesis:** Fire-wielding individuals or cautious travelers

KAMAGAMI

- **Concept:** Deities or spirits residing in natural elements
- **Skills:** Elemental Affinity, Blessings
- **Frailty:** Vulnerable to pollution or defilement of their element
- **Gear:** Embodiment of their natural domain
- **Goal:** Protect and maintain their natural realm
- **Motive:** Preserve balance and harmony
- **Nemesis:** Those who exploit or misuse their domains

KAMAITACHI

- **Concept:** Trio of weasel-like spirits associated with winds
- **Skills:** Speed, Cutting Winds
- **Frailty:** Vulnerable when winds are calm
- **Gear:** Sharp claws, swift movements
- **Goal:** Cause minor wounds or confusion
- **Motive:** Playful pranks or seek food
- **Nemesis:** Wind-manipulating individuals or those with strong barriers

KAMIKAKUSHI

- **Concept:** Phenomenon of mysterious disappear-ances
- **Skills:** Invisibility, Di-mensional Manipu-lation
- **Frailty:** Vulnerable to detection or seal-ing methods
- **Gear:** None
- **Goal:** Abduct and hide people
- **Motive:** Unknown, possibly fascination with human world
- **Nemesis:** Dimensional travelers or beings with detection abilities

KAMIKIRI

- **Concept:** Hair-cutting creature
- **Skills:** Stealth, Precision Cutting
- **Frailty:** Vulnerable to protective charms or hair talis-mans
- **Gear:** Small blades or shears
- **Goal:** Collect strands of human hair
- **Motive:** Seek hair for its nest or use in rituals
- **Nemesis:** People with strong protective measures or hair-enhancing abilities

KAPPA

- **Concept:** Mischievous water-dwelling creatures
- **Skills:** Swimming, Pranks
- **Frailty:** Vulnerable to spilling water from its head
- **Gear:** Water-filled dish on its head
- **Goal:** Pull pranks or challenge humans
- **Motive:** Seek amusement and food
- **Nemesis:** Skilled swimmers or clever humans

KIJO

- **Concept:** Seductive and dangerous female demon
- **Skills:** Charm, Deception
- **Frailty:** Vulnerable to purity or divine intervention
- **Gear:** Enchanting appearance, beguiling words
- **Goal:** Seduce and corrupt humans
- **Motive:** Seek pleasure or spread chaos
- **Nemesis:** Virtuous individuals or those with strong will

KITSUNE

- **Concept:** Cunning fox spirits
- **Skills:** Shape-shifting, Illusion
- **Frailty:** Vulnerable to certain chants or rituals
- **Gear:** None
- **Goal:** Protect their shrines or manipulate humans
- **Motive:** Gain power or amusement
- **Nemesis:** Skilled priests or holy relics

KONAKI-JIJI

- **Concept:** Old man youkai who cries like a baby
- **Skills:** Mimicry, Emotional Manipulation
- **Frailty:** Vulnerable to recognition or protective chants
- **Gear:** None
- **Goal:** Lure and deceive unsuspecting victims
- **Motive:** Seek amusement or feed on emotions
- **Nemesis:** Emotionally resilient individuals or those who see through its act

KUBIRE-ONI

- **Concept:** Headless demon or ogre
- **Skills:** Brute Strength, Fear-Inducing Roar
- **Frailty:** Vulnerable to sealing rituals or holy symbols
- **Gear:** None
- **Goal:** Spread fear and chaos
- **Motive:** Seek dominance or terrorize humans
- **Nemesis:** Skilled exorcists or brave warriors

KAWA-NO-KAMI

- **Concept:** River deities or spirits
- **Skills:** Water Manipulation, Communication
- **Frailty:** Vulnerable to pollution or desecration
- **Gear:** None
- **Goal:** Protect their domain and inhabitants
- **Motive:** Maintain the balance of nature
- **Nemesis:** Those who pollute or harm water sources

KAWA-USO

- **Concept:** River otter spirits known for pranks
- **Skills:** Mischief, Shapeshifting
- **Frailty:** Vulnerable to protective charms or water purification
- **Gear:** None
- **Goal:** Play pranks on humans and cause chaos
- **Motive:** Seek amusement or entertainment
- **Nemesis:** Those who outwit or out-prank them

KASHA

- **Concept:** Corpse-stealing creature
- **Skills:** Grave Desecration, Stealth
- **Frailty:** Vulnerable to protective barriers or sanctified ground
- **Gear:** None
- **Goal:** Steal corpses before they can be properly buried
- **Motive:** Unknown, possibly collecting remains for unknown purposes
- **Nemesis:** Guardians of burial sites or those protecting the dead

NUE

- **Concept:** Chimera-like creature with various animal parts
- **Skills:** Elemental Affinities, Shape-shifting
- **Frailty:** Vulnerable to certain elemental attacks
- **Gear:** None
- **Goal:** Cause chaos and confusion
- **Motive:** Seek dominance or play pranks
- **Nemesis:** Elemental specialists or skilled shape-shifters

NUKARUMI

- **Concept:** Female spirit appearing from the waist up in water
- **Skills:** Water Manipulation, Emotional Manifestation
- **Frailty:** Vulnerable to drying or containment
- **Gear:** Watery hands and upper body
- **Goal:** Emerge from bodies of water to interact with humans
- **Motive:** Seek connection or communication
- **Nemesis:** Water manipulators or those with abilities to control emotions

NOPPERA-BO

- **Concept:** Faceless ghostly figures
- **Skills:** Invisibility, Disguise
- **Frailty:** Vulnerable to light or certain charms
- **Gear:** None
- **Goal:** Frighten and unsettle humans
- **Motive:** Cause confusion and fear
- **Nemesis:** Sharp-eyed individuals or those unaffected by illusions

NURARI

- **Concept:** Youkai that lounges in unoccupied homes
- **Skills:** Stealth, Deception
- **Frailty:** Vulnerable when confronted or exposed to bright light
- **Gear:** None
- **Goal:** Claim unoccupied spaces and enjoy hospitality
- **Motive:** Seek comfort and luxury
- **Nemesis:** Vigilant homeowners or protective spirits

NURARIHYON

- **Concept:** Yokai that makes itself at home in empty houses
- **Skills:** Stealth, Deception
- **Frailty:** Vulnerable when confronted or exposed to bright light
- **Gear:** None
- **Goal:** Claim empty homes and spaces
- **Motive:** Seek comfort and convenience
- **Nemesis:** Vigilant home-owners or protective spirits

ONI

- **Concept:** Malevolent demons or ogres
- **Skills:** Strength, Intimidation
- **Frailty:** Vulnerable to sacred symbols or exorcism
- **Gear:** Clubs, spiked clubs, demonic masks
- **Goal:** Cause suffering and chaos
- **Motive:** Instill fear and exert dominance
- **Nemesis:** Powerful priests or brave warriors

RAIJU

- **Concept:** Creature associated with lightning
- **Skills:** Lightning Manipulation, Thunderstorm Control
- **Frailty:** Vulnerable to grounding or weather-controlling abilities
- **Gear:** None
- **Goal:** Harness and control thunderstorms
- **Motive:** Maintain balance or unleash chaos
- **Nemesis:** Storm manipulators or lightning-resistant beings

ROKUROKUBI

- **Concept:** Humanoid spirits with stretchable necks
- **Skills:** Neck Extension, Stealth
- **Frailty:** Vulnerable when neck is extended
- **Gear:** None
- **Goal:** Observe humans or cause confusion
- **Motive:** Seek amusement or explore
- **Nemesis:** Observant individuals or those with anti-magic abilities

SATORI

- **Concept:** Mind-reading creature
- **Skills:** Telepathy, Mind Reading
- **Frailty:** Vulnerable to psychic barriers or strong wills
- **Gear:** None
- **Goal:** Learn the thoughts and secrets of humans
- **Motive:** Seek knowledge or manipulate individuals
- **Nemesis:** Those with strong mental defenses or psychic powers

SHIRIME

- **Concept:** Creature with an eye in place of its anus
- **Skills:** Startling Gaze, Stealth
- **Frailty:** Vulnerable to salt or counter-illusion
- **Gear:** None
- **Goal:** Shock and surprise victims
- **Motive:** Seek amusement or disturb humans
- **Nemesis:** Those unaffected by its gaze or those with strong wills

TENGU
- **Concept:** Bird-like creatures with supernatural powers
- **Skills:** Flight, Martial Arts
- **Frailty:** Vulnerable to talismans or divine intervention
- **Gear:** Long-nosed masks, magical fans
- **Goal:** Maintain balance in nature or teach valuable lessons
- **Motive:** Promote harmony or discipline
- **Nemesis:** Skilled martial artists or divine beings

TESSO
- **Concept:** Vengeful spirit of a mistreated priest or monk
- **Skills:** Curse Casting, Disruptive Presence
- **Frailty:** Vulnerable to purification or redemption rituals
- **Gear:** None
- **Goal:** Exact revenge for past mistreatment
- **Motive:** Seek justice or restitution
- **Nemesis:** Compassionate individuals or those seeking to right wrongs

TANUKI
- **Concept:** Playful shape-shifting raccoon dog spirits
- **Skills:** Shape-shifting, Misdirection
- **Frailty:** Vulnerable to charms or spells
- **Gear:** None
- **Goal:** Cause mischief or seek comfort
- **Motive:** Enjoyment and freedom
- **Nemesis:** Protective deities or skilled exorcists

UMIBOZU
- **Concept:** Sea spirit that causes storms
- **Skills:** Water Manipulation, Tempest Creation
- **Frailty:** Vulnerable to certain chants or rituals
- **Gear:** None
- **Goal:** Create treacherous seas and storms
- **Motive:** Seek chaos and destruction
- **Nemesis:** Skilled sailors or divine protectors

YAMABIKO

- **Concept:** Echo spirits that mimic human voices
- **Skills:** Echo Mimicry, Illusion
- **Frailty:** Vulnerable to silence or counter-illusion
- **Gear:** None
- **Goal:** Echo and repeat human sounds
- **Motive:** Seek interaction or amusement
- **Nemesis:** Skilled ventriloquists or sound manipulators

YUKI-ONNA

- **Concept:** Spirit associated with snowstorms
- **Skills:** Cold Manipulation, Illusion
- **Frailty:** Vulnerable to warmth or heat-based attacks
- **Gear:** None
- **Goal:** Ensnare travelers in blizzards
- **Motive:** Seek companionship or revenge
- **Nemesis:** Fire-wielding individuals or those with strong willpower

YOKAI

- **Concept:** Mysterious shape-shifting spirits
- **Skills:** Shapeshifting, Illusion
- **Frailty:** Vulnerable to pure iron
- **Gear:** None
- **Goal:** To trick or deceive humans
- **Motive:** Mischievous or malevolent intentions
- **Nemesis:** Talismans or individuals skilled in exorcism

YUREI

- **Concept:** Ghostly spirits of the deceased
- **Skills:** Manifestation, Frightening Aura
- **Frailty:** Vulnerable to prayers or appeasement
- **Gear:** None
- **Goal:** Find peace or seek revenge
- **Motive:** Resolve unfinished business or seek justice
- **Nemesis:** Skilled mediums or compassionate priests

ZASHIKI-WARASHI

- **Concept:** Child spirits that bring fortune or misfortune
- **Skills:** Luck Manipulation, Playful Behavior
- **Frailty:** Vulnerable when neglected or angered
- **Gear:** None
- **Goal:** Influence the household's luck
- **Motive:** Seek attention and care
- **Nemesis:** Neglectful or hostile individuals

APPENDIX A: CULTURAL INSIGHTS AND GLOSSARY

Historical Context: Feudal Japan was a time of samurai, warlords, and mysterious spirits. Dive into the history of warring clans, honor codes, and the rise of noble families that shape the backdrop of your adventures.

Cultural Traditions: From the elegant art of the tea ceremony to the intricate world of ikebana (flower arranging), learn about the customs that defined daily life in old Japan. Understanding these traditions can guide your interactions with NPCs and reveal hidden clues.

Spiritual Beliefs: Ghosts, demons, and shapeshifters are not just fantasy here; they're rooted in Japanese spiritual beliefs. Discover the rich mythology of yokai, the supernatural creatures that inhabit the world around you.

Samurai Code: Uncover the principles of bushido, the way of the samurai. Loyalty, honor, and duty were central tenets that governed the lives of these noble warriors. Your character's actions can reflect or challenge these ideals.

Language and Honorifics: Get a grip on common Japanese phrases, honorifics, and titles. Addressing NPCs with respect or familiarity can influence how they respond to you.

Festivals and Celebrations: Participate in vibrant festivals like Tanabata, where wishes are written on paper and hung on bamboo, or Obon, a time to honor the spirits of the deceased. These celebrations provide unique opportunities for interaction and adventure.

Japanese Folklore: Delve into the captivating world of Japanese folklore. Learn about famous legends like Momotaro, the Peach Boy, and Tsukuyomi, the Moon God. These stories can provide inspiration and context for your adventures.

APPENDIX B: GLOSSARY

This glossary provides a comprehensive overview of terms related to the kwaidan genre and feudal Japan, encompassing both supernatural elements and cultural aspects that enrich the storytelling experience.

A

Akashita: A ghostly hand that reaches up from beneath tatami mats, often used to startle or shock.

Amanojaku: Mischievous demons that enjoy causing chaos and confusion.

Ancestral Spirits: Believed to be the spirits of deceased ancestors who continue to influence and protect their living descendants.

B

Bakufu: A feudal military government that ruled Japan from the 12th to the 19th centuries.

Bunraku: Traditional Japanese puppet theater.

Bushi: A samurai warrior or a person belonging to the warrior class.

C

Chonmage: A traditional Japanese hairstyle associated with samurai, characterized by a shaved pate and a topknot.

D

Daimyo: Feudal lords who governed specific territories in feudal Japan.

Edo: The former name of Tokyo, serving as the political and cultural center of Japan during the Edo period.

E

Edo Period: A time of relative peace and stability in Japan from 1603 to 1868, characterized by the rule of the Tokugawa shogunate and isolation from the outside world.

F

Feudal System: A hierarchical social structure where power and land ownership were concentrated in the hands of a ruling class, mainly samurai and daimyo.

G

Geisha: Skilled entertainers who perform traditional Japanese arts, often including dance, music, and conversation.

Genroku Era: A period of cultural flourishing during the Edo period, known for its artistic and literary achievements.

Geta: Traditional Japanese wooden sandals, often worn with kimono.

H

Hanami: The practice of enjoying the beauty of cherry blossoms (sakura) during spring.

Heian Period: A historical period from the late 8th to the late 12th century, characterized by the flourishing of literature and culture in the imperial court.

I

Inro: A small, multi-compartmental container used to hold personal belongings, often worn by samurai.

Irezumi: Traditional Japanese tattoo art.

J

Jorogumo: A spider that can transform into a beautiful woman, often used to seduce and trap victims.

Joruri: The narrative or dialogue in Bunraku puppet theater.

Jukujo: A type of ghost or spirit that embodies an elderly woman.

Junihitoe: An elaborate and multilayered kimono worn by noblewomen in the Heian period.

K

Kabuki: A traditional form of Japanese theater known for its elaborate makeup, costumes, and dramatic performances.

Kamaitachi: A trio of weasel-like spirits associated with winds, known to cause mysterious cuts or wounds.

Kamikakushi: The phenomenon of people mysteriously disappearing, often attributed to supernatural causes.

Kamidana: A household Shinto shrine that enshrines ancestral spirits and guardian deities.

Kappa: Water-dwelling creatures resembling turtles or amphibians, known for their mischievous nature.

Karuta: Traditional Japanese playing cards.

Katana: A traditional Japanese sword, often associated with samurai warriors.

Kimon: The formal clothing worn by samurai, featuring a distinctive crest.

Kimono: Traditional Japanese clothing worn by men, women, and children, characterized by its T-shaped structure and wide sleeves.

Koto: A traditional Japanese stringed musical instrument.

Kwaidan: A genre of Japanese supernatural and ghost stories.

L

Lantern Festival: An annual festival held to honor deceased ancestors, often involving the lighting of lanterns.

M

Meiji Restoration: The period of political and social upheaval in Japan during the late 19th century, leading to the modernization of the country.

Miko: Shrine maidens who perform rituals and ceremonies at Shinto shrines.

Mokumokuren: A youkai that appears on torn, worn-out fusuma (sliding doors) and tatami mats.

Mononoke: Malevolent spirits or demons that bring misfortune or harm.

N

Nihonshu: Traditional Japanese rice wine, commonly known as sake.

Noh: Traditional Japanese theater characterized by its slow and stylized performances, often featuring masked actors.

Noppera-bo: Faceless ghostly figures, often appearing as normal individuals until revealing their smooth, featureless visages.

Nue: A chimera-like creature with the head of a monkey, body of a tanuki, legs of a tiger, and a snake for a tail.

Nurarihyon: A youkai that enters empty homes, sits down, and makes itself at home.

O

Oni: Malevolent demons or ogres that come in various forms and sizes, often depicted with vividly colored skin.

Oyabun: The leader or head of a yakuza crime syndicate.

R

Raiju: A creature associated with lightning, often depicted as a beast with the ability to control thunderstorms.

Rokurokubi: Humanoid spirits with the ability to stretch their necks, often appearing as normal individuals until revealing their supernatural trait.

S

Sakabashira: A ritual where a human sacrifice is entombed within the foundations of a new building to ensure its stability.

Samurai: Members of a warrior class in feudal Japan, known for their strict code of conduct, Bushido.

Satori: A creature with the ability to read human minds and reveal their thoughts.

Shogunate: A feudal military government led by a shogun, the de facto ruler of Japan.

Shrine Architecture: Traditional Japanese architecture used in the construction of Shinto shrines, characterized by its torii gate, honden (main hall), and haiden (worship hall).

Shuriken: Traditional Japanese throwing weapons, often in the form of star-shaped blades.

Swordsmithing: The art of crafting traditional Japanese swords, often passed down through generations.

T

Tatami: Traditional Japanese flooring material made of woven straw, often used as a base for sleeping, sitting, or other activities.

Tengu: Bird-like creatures with supernatural powers, often depicted with long noses.

Tokonoma: A recessed alcove in a traditional Japanese room used to display art or other decorative items.

Tsukumogami: Inanimate objects that come to life after 100 years of existence, often becoming mischievous spirits.

U

Umibozu: A sea spirit known for causing treacherous storms and tempests.

Y

Yamabiko: Echo spirits that mimic human voices, often found in mountainous areas.

Yokai: Supernatural creatures and spirits found in Japanese folklore, encompassing a wide range of beings with various abilities and forms.

Yurei: Ghostly spirits of the deceased, often depicted as pale figures in white burial kimono.

Yuki-onna: A spirit associated with snowstorms, often depicted as a beautiful woman with the power to freeze humans.

Zashiki-warashi: Child spirits that bring fortune or misfortune to households, often depicted as mischievous pranksters.

APPENDIX C: INSPIRATIONAL MEDIA

Here are some recommended readings and media that can further immerse you in the world of feudal Japan, its culture, and supernatural elements:

BOOKS

- "Kwaidan: Stories and Studies of Strange Things" by Lafcadio Hearn
- "The Book of Yokai: Mysterious Creatures of Japanese Folklore" by Michael Dylan Foster
- "Shogun" by James Clavell
- "Musashi" by Eiji Yoshikawa
- "The Tale of Genji" by Murasaki Shikibu
- "The Samurai's Garden" by Gail Tsukiyama
- "The Night Parade of One Hundred Demons: A Field Guide to Japanese Yokai" by Matthew Meyer

MOVIES AND TV SHOWS

- "Kwaidan" (1964) - A classic Japanese horror anthology film.
- "Princess Mononoke" (1997) - An animated fantasy film by Studio Ghibli that explores the relationship between humans and nature.
- "Rurouni Kenshin" (1996-1998) - An anime series set during the Meiji era, following a former assassin's journey for redemption.
- "Throne of Blood" (1957) - A film adaptation of Shakespeare's "Macbeth," set in feudal Japan and directed by Akira Kurosawa.
- "Mushishi" (2005-2006) - An anime series that delves into the interactions between humans and supernatural creatures called Mushi.
- "Onmyoji" (2001) - A fantasy film about an onmyoji (a practitioner of traditional Japanese esoteric cosmology) in the Heian period.
- "Sword of the Stranger" (2007) - An anime film featuring a ronin's encounter with a young boy and his quest for revenge.

VIDEO GAMES

- "Ghost of Tsushima" (2020) - An action-adventure game set in feudal Japan, where you play as a samurai warrior.
- "Nioh" (2017) - An action RPG inspired by Japanese history and mythology, featuring intense combat and supernatural elements.
- "Okami" (2006) - An action-adventure game where you control a wolf goddess, drawing on Japanese mythology and art style.
- "Way of the Samurai" series - A series of games that allow players to navigate feudal Japan's conflicts as a wandering samurai.

DOCUMENTARIES

- "Japan: Memoirs of a Secret Empire" - A PBS documentary series that explores Japan's history, including its feudal period.
- "Kaidan: Ghosts and Demons of Japan" - A documentary that delves into Japanese ghost stories and folklore.

ONLINE RESOURCES

- Yokai.com - A website dedicated to Japanese yokai (supernatural creatures), complete with illustrations and descriptions.
- The Samurai Archives - An online resource for historical information about samurai, warfare, and culture.
- Kyoto National Museum Virtual Gallery - Explore virtual exhibitions showcasing traditional Japanese art and artifacts.

KWAIDAN!

LONER EXPRESS RULES

LONER is a minimalist Solo Role Playing Game designed to be played with only one character (the Protagonist).
Any action is resolved by asking a closed question to the Oracle.

EVERYTHING IS A CHARACTER!

In *Loner* Non-Playing Characters (NPCs), Foes, Organizations, Monsters, and even relevant objects like vehicles are characters too!

Your Protagonist is described by some fixed traits:

- **Name**: the name should be iconic and consistent with the tone and setting of the story
- **Concept**: A concise description of the character's profession, background, and abilities. The best are adjective-name pairings, like "Venturous Smuggler" or "Child Prodigy".
- **Skills (x2)**: abilities not necessarily character-specific but not characteristics common to all. "Smart" is not a skill, "Engine Whisperer" is.
- **Frailty**: something that could potentially get in the way of the character, either physically, mentally, or socially.
- **Gear (x2)**: particular equipment supplied to the character in coherence with the setting. Everyday items are taken for granted and do not fall under this trait.
- **Goal**: the long-term objective.
- **Motive**: what drives the pursuit of the goal.
- **Nemesis**: a person or organization that hinders the protagonist. It can emerge during the first game sessions, it may or may or not be the direct antagonist of the story, ready to appear to make life even more difficult
- **Luck**: The measure of a character's ability to avoid ill fortune or an inauspicious outcome. It applies only in Conflicts and automatically recharges when they end. Luck starts and caps at 6.

These **traits** are described by **tags**, descriptive words or phrases that can identify anything in the game world. Even the **details** of the environment in which the action moves and the **condition** (physical or mental) of the characters are tags.

They are qualitative representations. **They are not quantitative measures.**

CONSULTING THE ORACLE

When you need to test your expectations you'll ask the Oracle a closed question.

You'll need 2d6 in one color (**Chance Dice**), and 2d6 in another (**Risk Dice**).

To resolve a closed question, roll one **Chance Die** and one **Risk Die**:

- If the Chance Die is highest, the answer is **Yes**.
- If the Risk Die is highest, the answer is **No**.
- If both are low (3 or less), add a **but....**
- If both are high (4 or more), add an **and....**
- If both are equal, the answer is **Yes, but....** Add a point to the **Twist Counter**.

ADVANTAGE AND DISADVANTAGE

If circumstances or positive tags grant an advantage, add a **Chance Die** to the roll. Otherwise, when hindrances or negative tag cause a disadvantage, add a **Risk Die**. In both cases keep only the higher die of the added type when you check the roll.

Consider tags **intuitively and not quantitatively.**

TWISTS

The Twist Counter is a measure of the rising tension in the narrative. At the beginning is set to 0. Every time a double throw (dice are equal) happens, add 1 to the Counter. If the Counter is below three, consider the answer as "**Yes, but...**". Otherwise a **Twist** happens and resets the Counter.

Roll 2d6 and consult the following Twist Table to determine what kind of twist happens.

D6	Subject	Action
⚀	A third party	Appears
⚁	The hero	Alters the location
⚂	An encounter	Helps the hero
⚃	A physical event	Hinders the hero
⚄	An emotional event	Changes the goal
⚅	An object	Ends the scene

CONFLICTS

A *Conflict* is any situation in which opponents clash, attacking, defending, or wearing each other down in order to win. This applies both in a practical and metaphorical sense.

Conflicts can be resolved in different ways depending on preferences and context:

1. Ask a single closed question. The Oracle's answer determines the outcome of the conflict.
2. Ask a series of closed questions to resolve current single actions.
3. Use the rules of Harm & Luck below.

Note that the Twist Counter **does not apply** to Harm & Luck.

If the conflict is resolved by applying damage to the Luck trait, roll the dice to determine whether the protagonist causes damage to the opponent or suffers damage due to counterattack or failed defense. The rolls are player facing only.

The damage reduces the Luck of the target, whether protagonist or NPC. When the Luck runs out, the character has lost the conflict.

Answer	Do you get what you want?	Harm
Yes, and...	You get what you want, and something else.	Cause 3
Yes...	You get what you want.	Cause 2
Yes, but...	You get what you want, but at a cost.	Cause 1
No, but...	You don't get what you want, but it's not a total loss.	Take 1
No...	You don't get what you were after.	Take 2
No, and...	You don't get what you want, and things get worse.	Take 3

DETERMINE THE MOOD OF THE NEXT SCENE

At the end of the current scene you can roll 1d6 and consult the table on the side:

OPEN-ENDED QUESTION OR GET INSPIRED

To answer an Open-Ended question, roll 1d6 once on each of the following tables (roll at least a verb and a noun, adjectives are optional).

D6	Next Scene
⚀ - ⚂	Dramatic scene
⚃ - ⚄	Quiet Scene
⚅	Meanwhile...

WHEN THE STORY ENDS

At the end of the adventure you may add another trait to the character. It is better that this is related to how the story just ended and can be either a Skill, Gear, a new Frailty, or even a new Nemesis! You can also modify an existing trait to better represent an enhanced expertise.

Also update the list of **NPCs**, **Locations**, and **Events** that may show up again in future adventures.

VERBS

	⚀	⚁	⚂
⚀	inject	pass	own
⚁	continue	learn	ask
⚂	develop	behave	replace
⚃	share	hand	play
⚄	face	expand	found
⚅	trip	want	miss

	⚃	⚄	⚅
⚀	divide	bury	borrow
⚁	multiply	receive	imagine
⚂	damage	collect	turn
⚃	explain	improve	cough
⚄	gather	prefer	belong
⚅	dry	employ	destroy

NOUNS

	⚀	⚁	⚂
⚀	cause	stage	change
⚁	front	event	home
⚂	prose	motion	trade
⚃	instrument	friend	talk
⚄	word	morning	edge
⚅	key	income	use
	⚃	⚄	⚅
⚀	verse	thrill	spot
⚁	bag	measure	birth
⚂	memory	chance	drop
⚃	liquid	fact	price
⚄	room	system	camp
⚅	humor	statement	argument

ADJECTIVES

	⚀	⚁	⚂
⚀	frequent	faulty	obscene
⚁	ethereal	sophisticated	rightful
⚂	descriptive	insidious	poor
⚃	silky	worthless	fixed
⚄	quiet	stormy	spooky
⚅	magnificent	arrogant	unhealthy

	⚃	⚄	⚅
⚀	scarce	rigid	long-term
⚁	knowledge-able	astonishing	ordinary
⚂	proud	reflective	amusing
⚃	loose	willing	cold
⚄	delirious	innate	late
⚅	enormous	truculent	charming

Need more in-depth explanations of the rules? The **Core Rules** are available,

Need ready-made hints and materials (NPCs, Locations, Factions and Adventure Seeds)? **Loner Complete** offers 12 Adventure Packs covering as many genres from fantasy to science fiction, horror to westerns, and more.

Find the Core and Complete Rules at:

- **itch.io:** https://zeruhur.itch.io/loner-2nd-edition
- **DriveThruRPG:**
  - https://www.drivethrurpg.com/product/427674/Loner--Core-Rules-2nd-Edition
  - https://www.drivethrurpg.com/product/456768/Loner-Complete